WE ARE ALL ME

A TOON BOOK BY

JORDAN CRANE

For Of To
Rebecca

Editorial Director: FRANÇOISE MOULY
Book Design: J.Crane & FRANÇOISE MOULY
JORDAN CRANE's artwork was created using pen, ink, and tablet.

A TOON BOOK

All our books are Smyth Sewn (the highest library-quality binding available) and printed with soy-based inks on acid-free wood free paper harvested from responsible sources. Printed in China by C&C Offset Printing Co., Ltd. Distributed to the trade by Consortium Book Sales; orders (800) 283-3572; orderentry@perseusbooks.com; www.cbsd.com.
Library of Congress Cataloging-in-Publication Data: Crane, Jordan, 1973- author, illustrator.
We are all me: a TOON book / by Jordan Crane. New York: TOON Books, 2018
Summary: "A poetic and lyrical picture book, bursting with color, about our interdependent world, from cell to self and seed to sky." — Provided by publisher. Identifiers: LCCN 2018000545 | ISBN 9781943145355
Subjects: LCSH: Graphic Novels. | CYAC: Graphic novels. | Life (Biology) - Fiction.
Classification: LCC PZ7.7.C74 We 2018 | DDC 741.5/973-dc23
ISBN: 978-1-943145-35-5
18 19 20 21 22 23 C&C 10 9 8 7 6 5 4 3 2 1

www.TOON-BOOKS.com

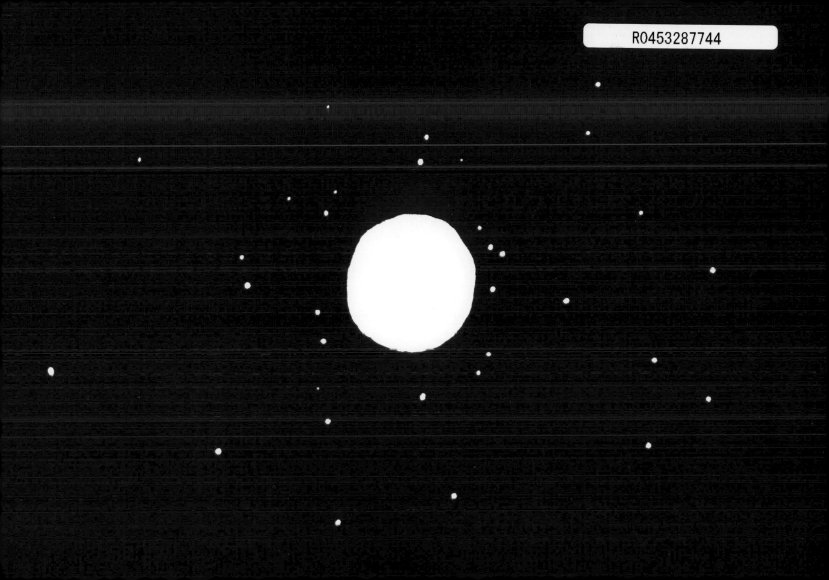

RO453287744

I AM
ONE

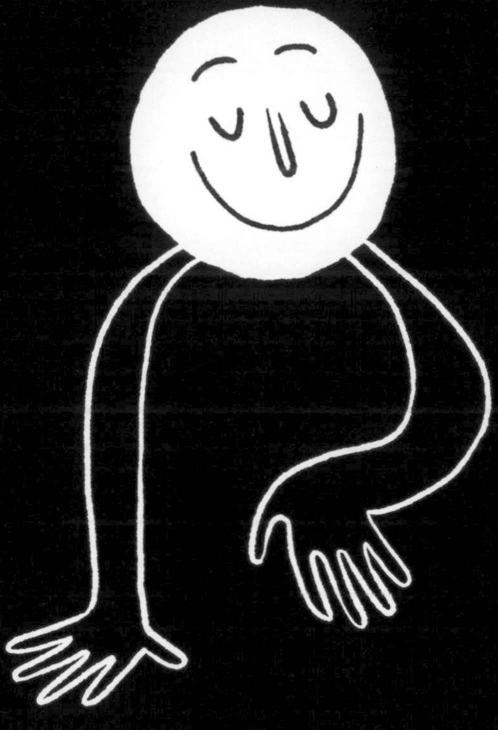

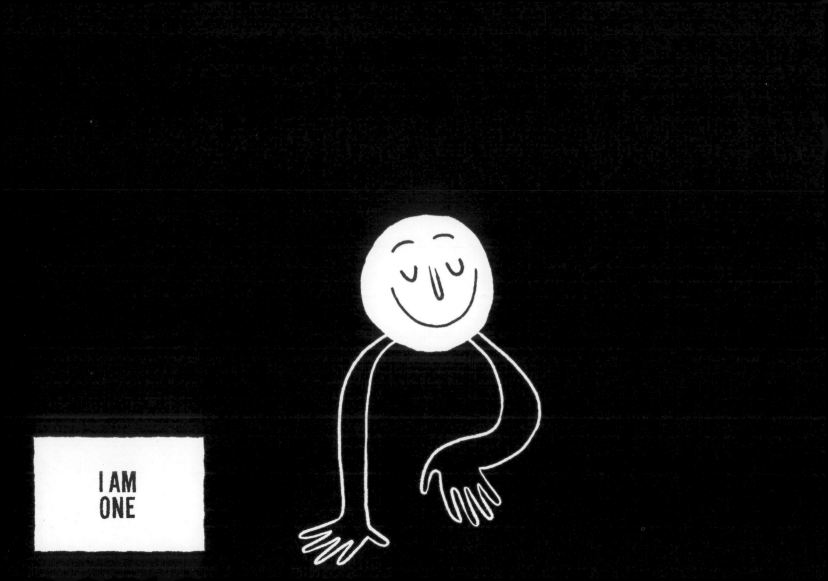

HERE IN A BODY

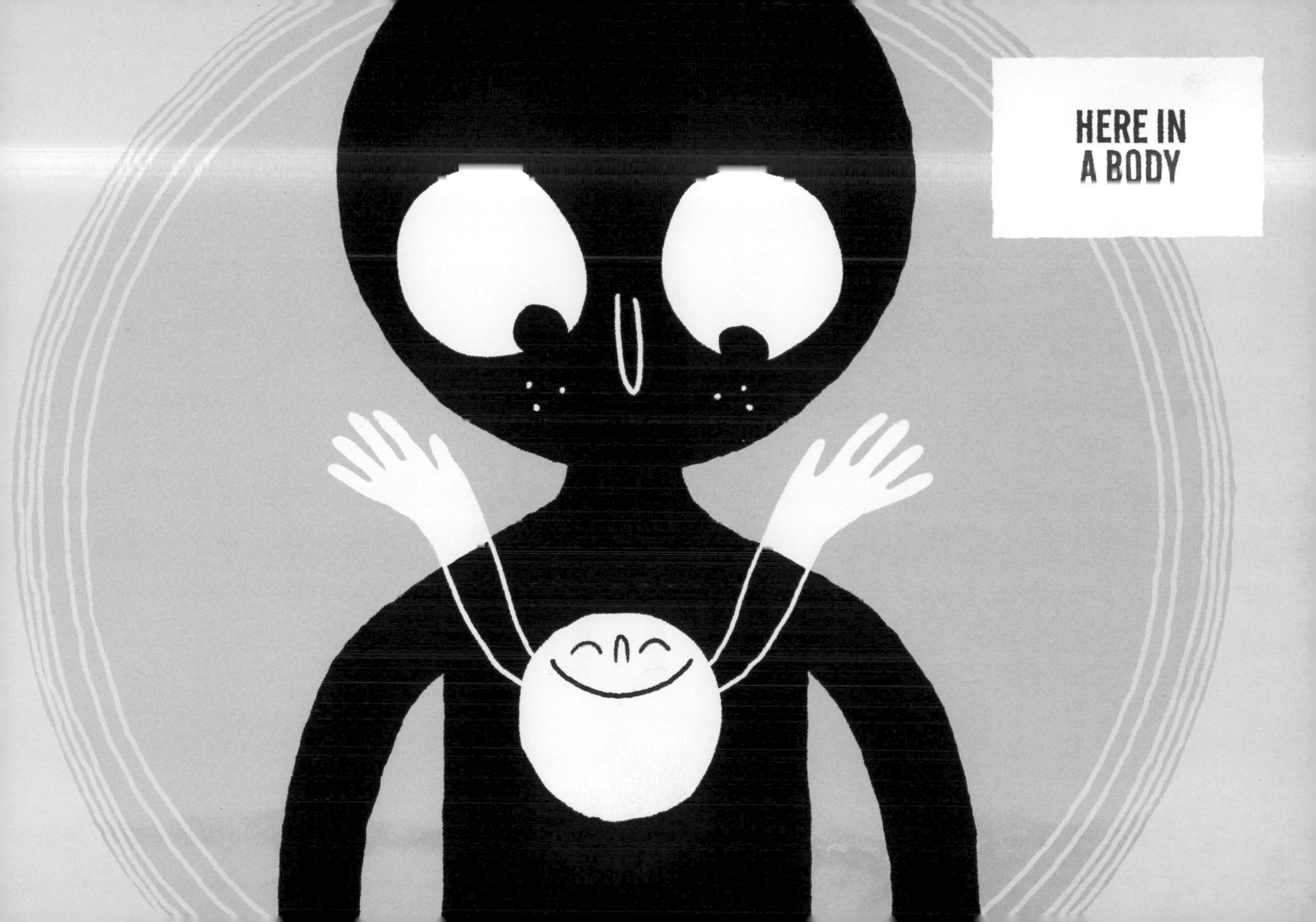

ALIVE IN A WORLD

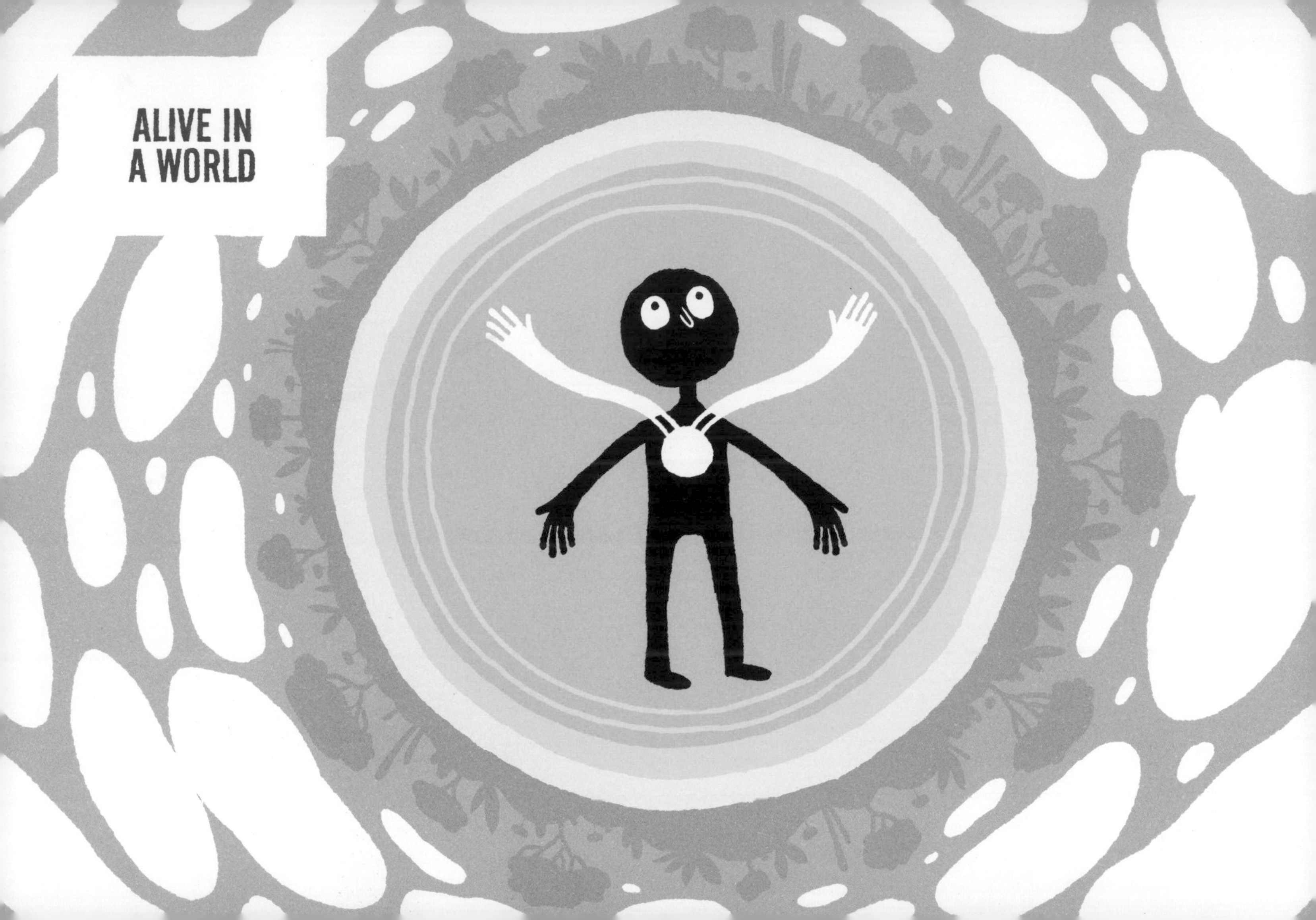

MADE
OF AIR

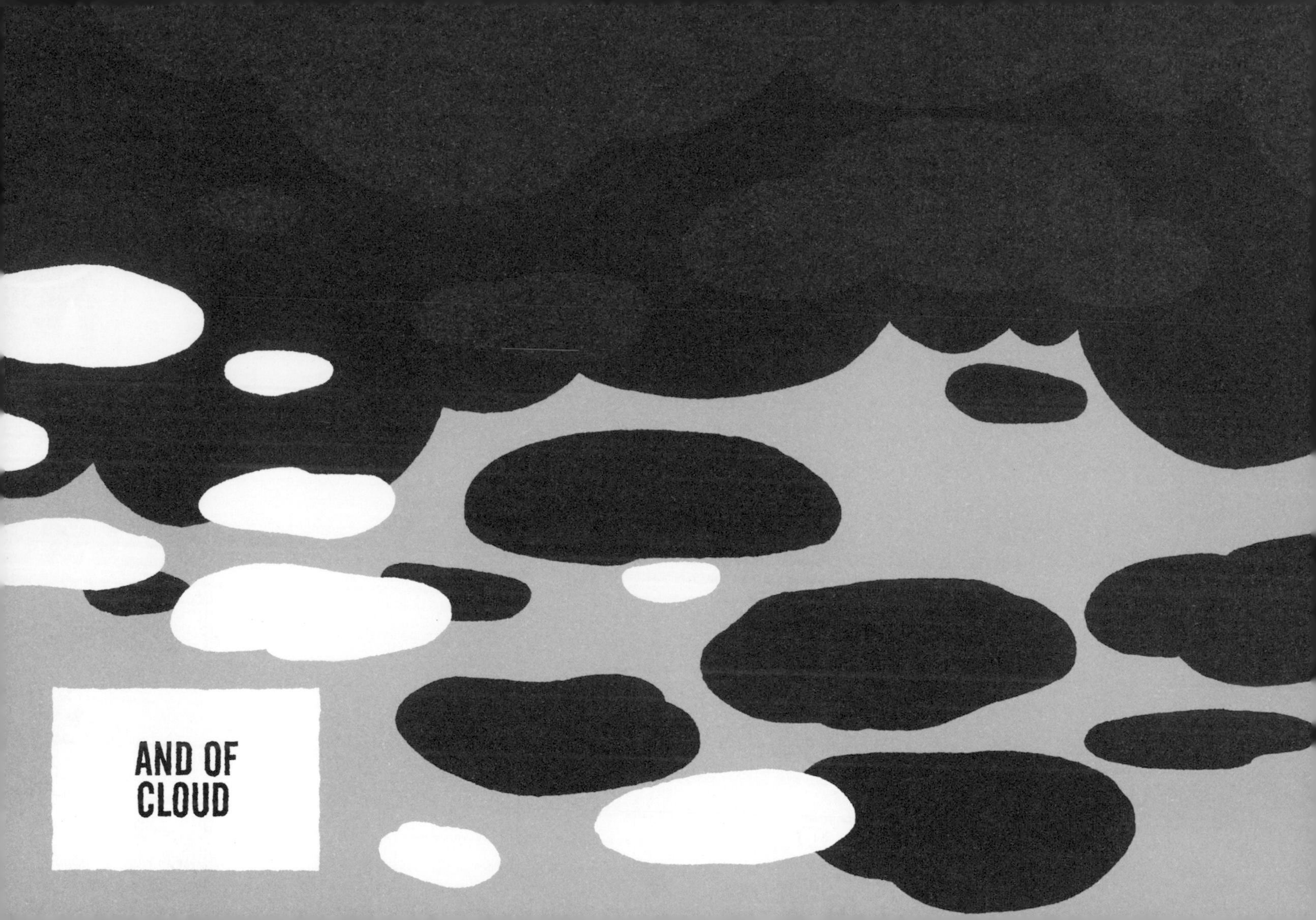
AND OF
CLOUD

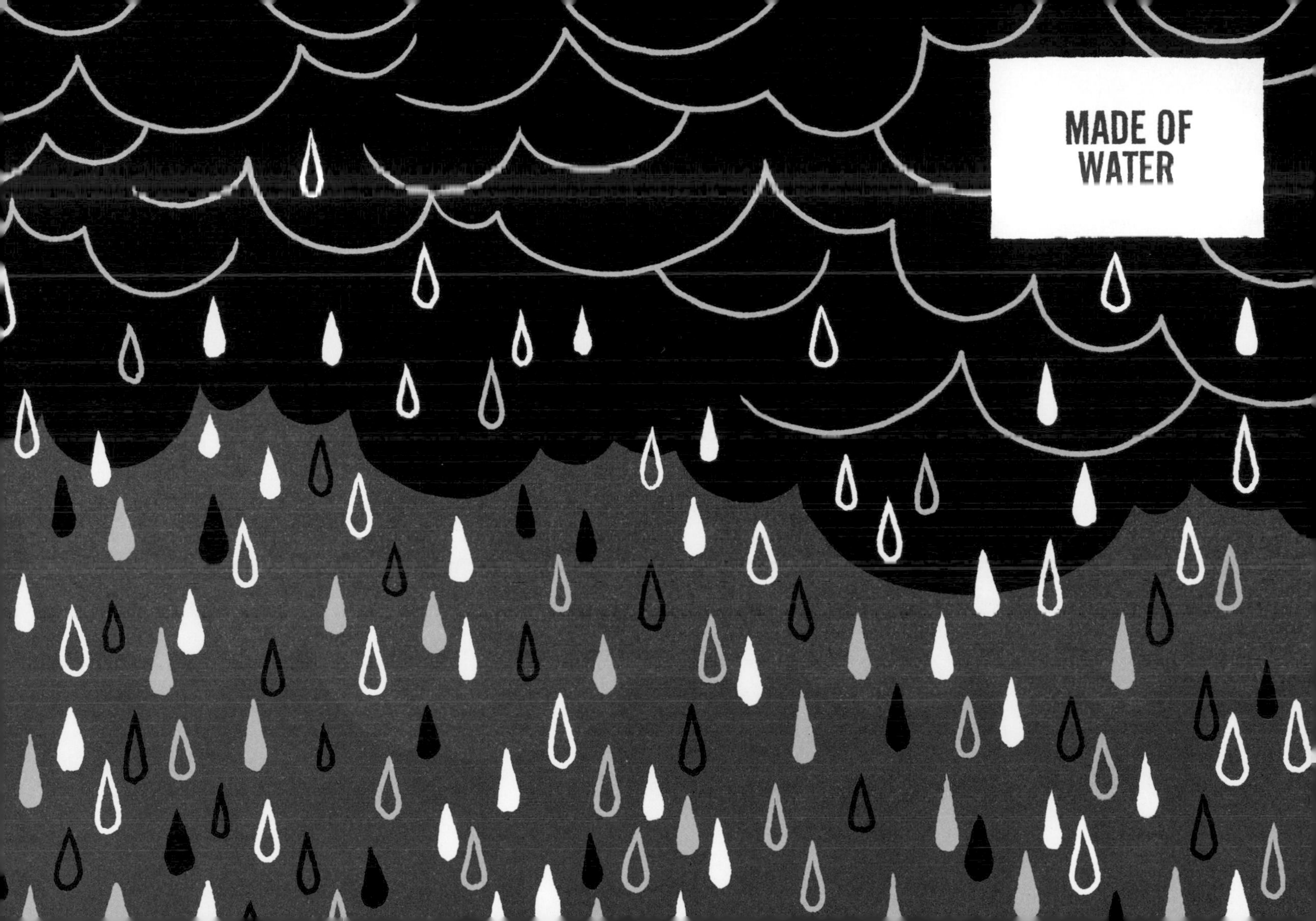
MADE OF WATER

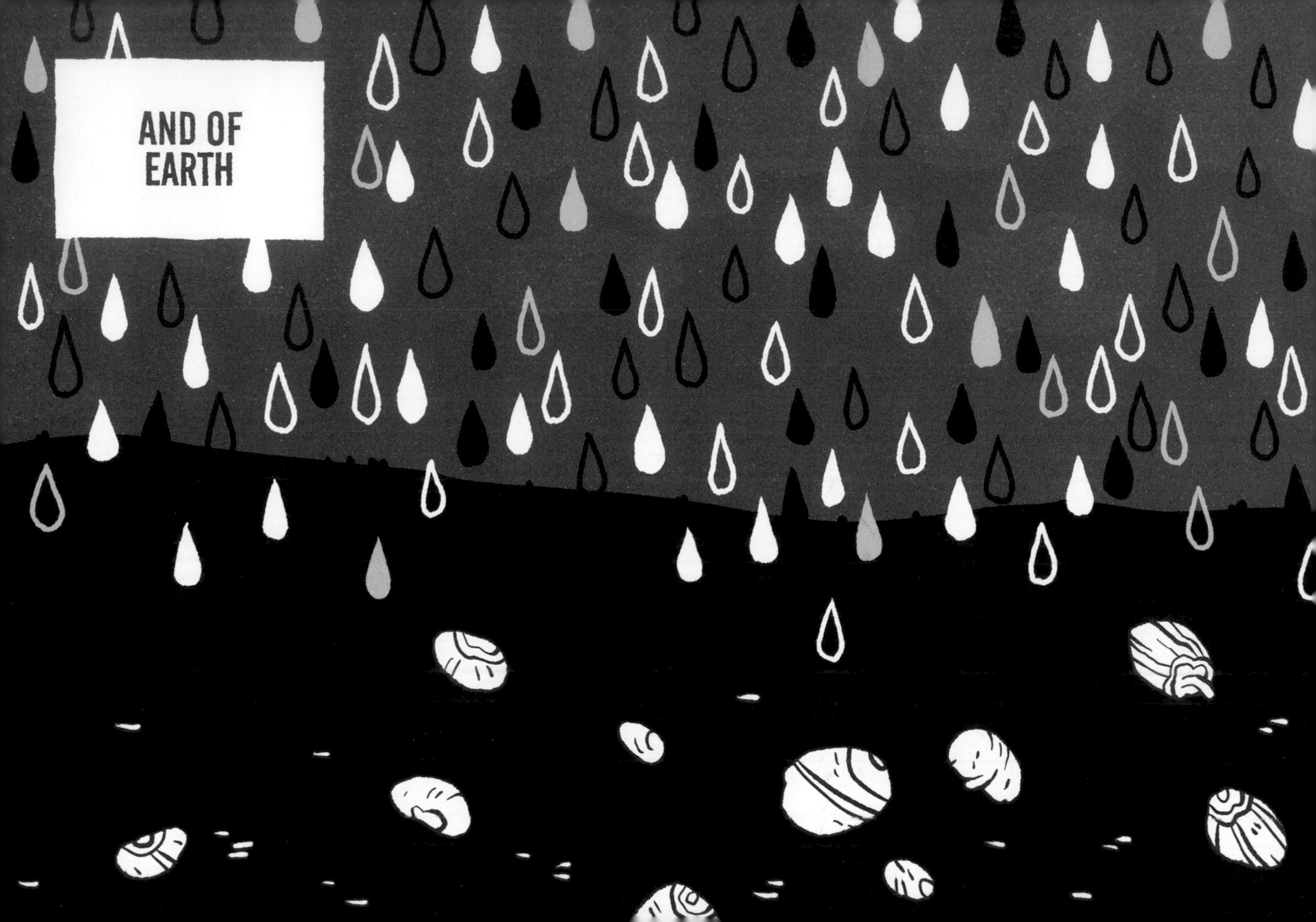
AND OF
EARTH

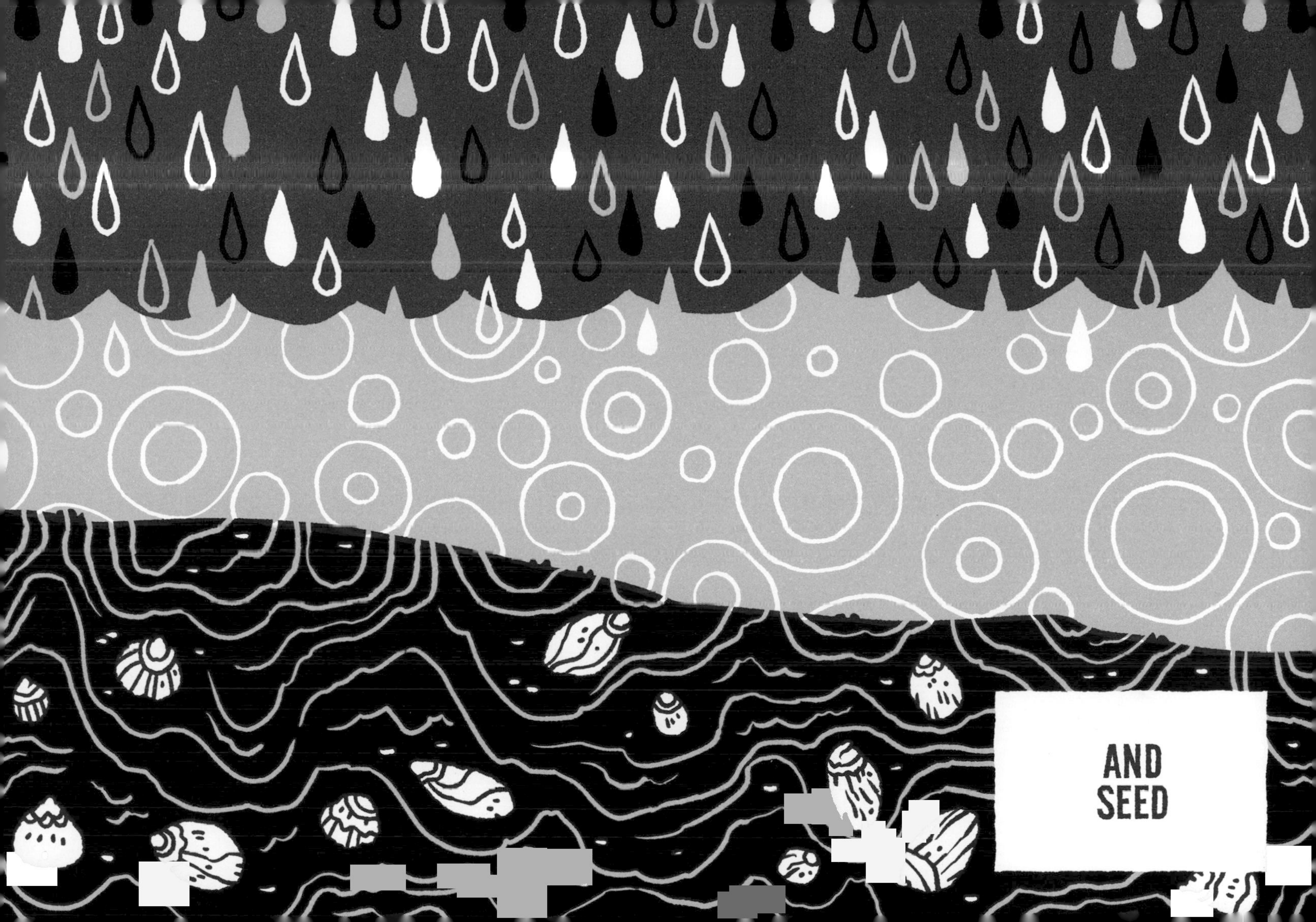
AND
SEED

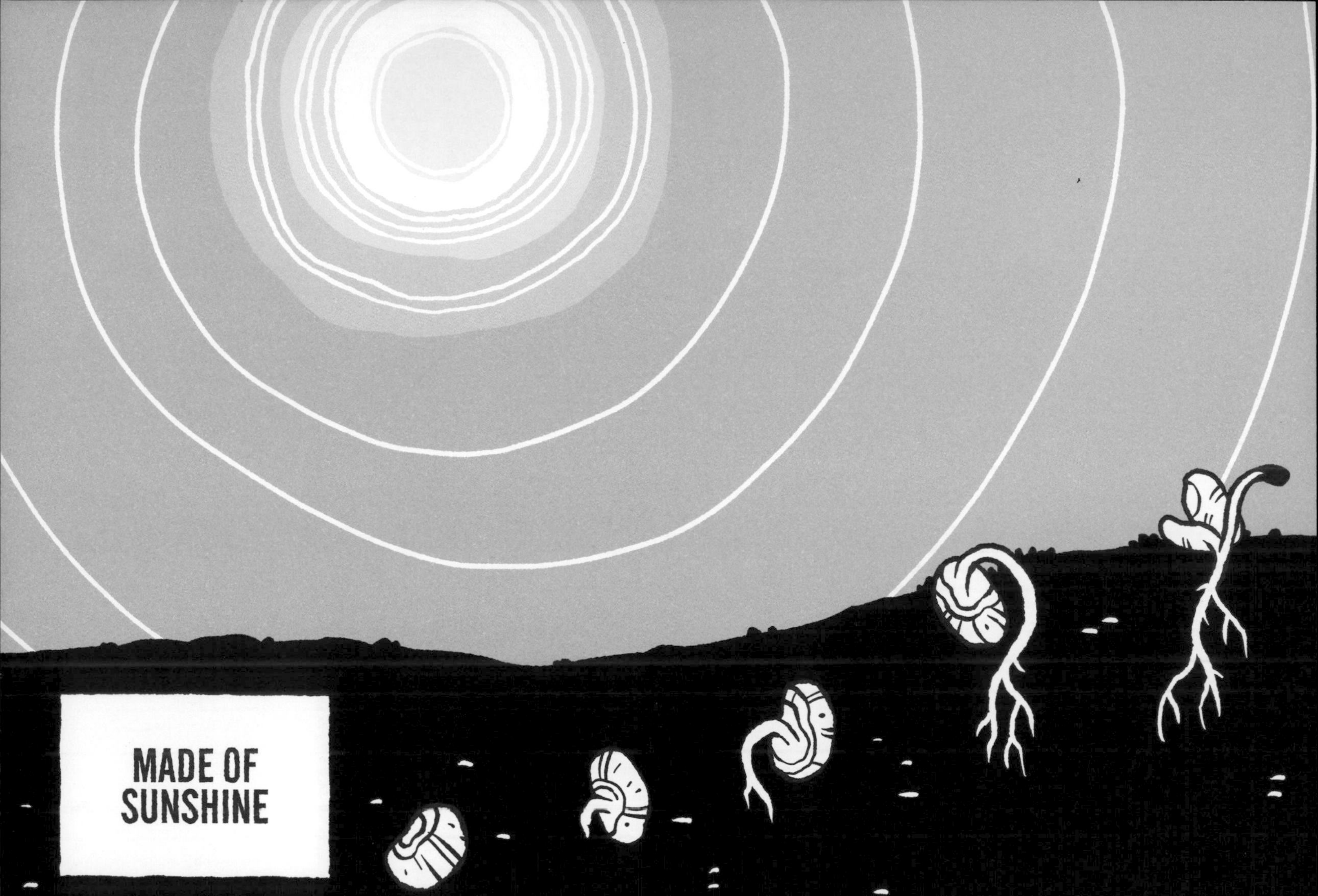
MADE OF
SUNSHINE

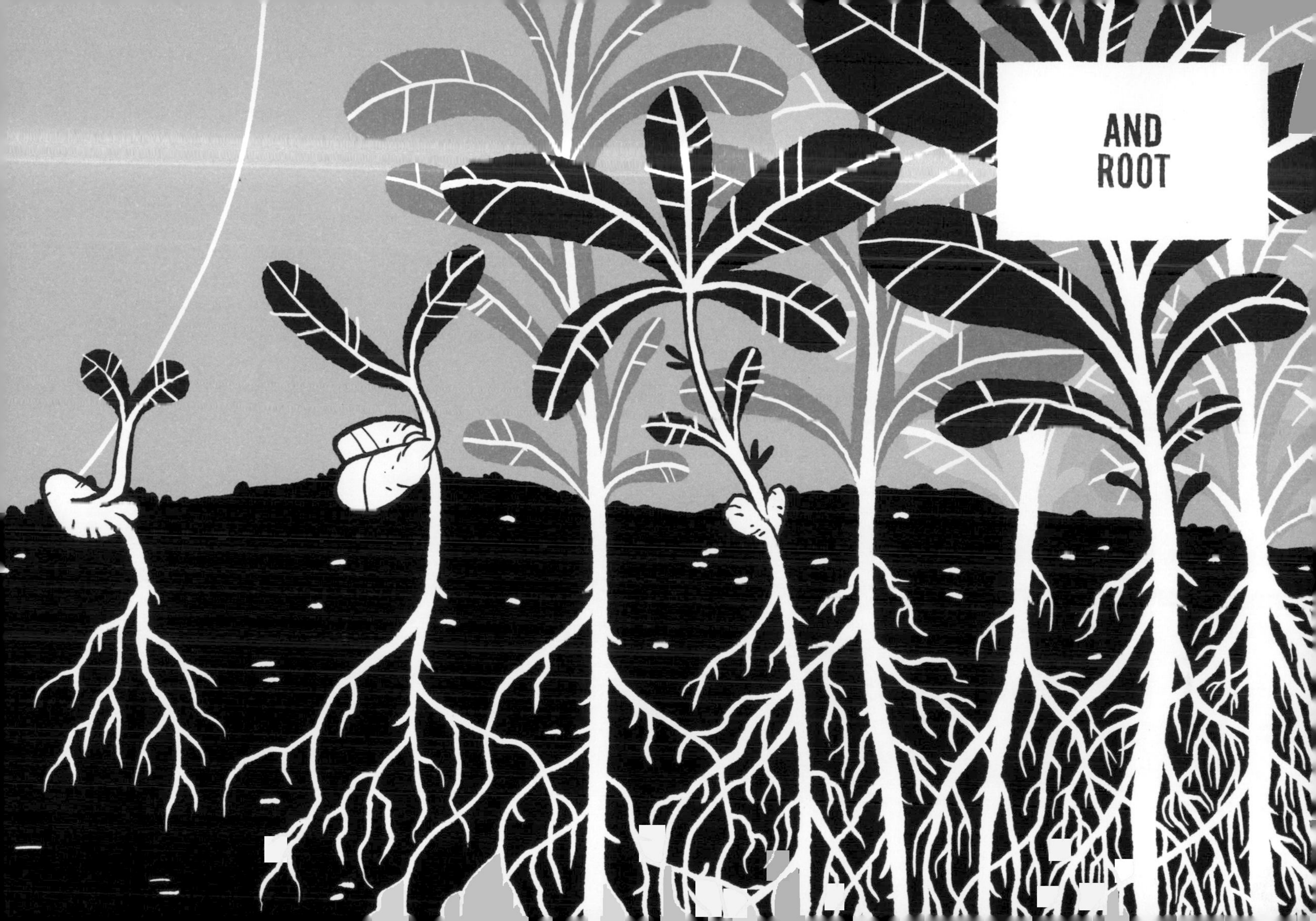
AND
ROOT

OF LEAF AND FRUIT

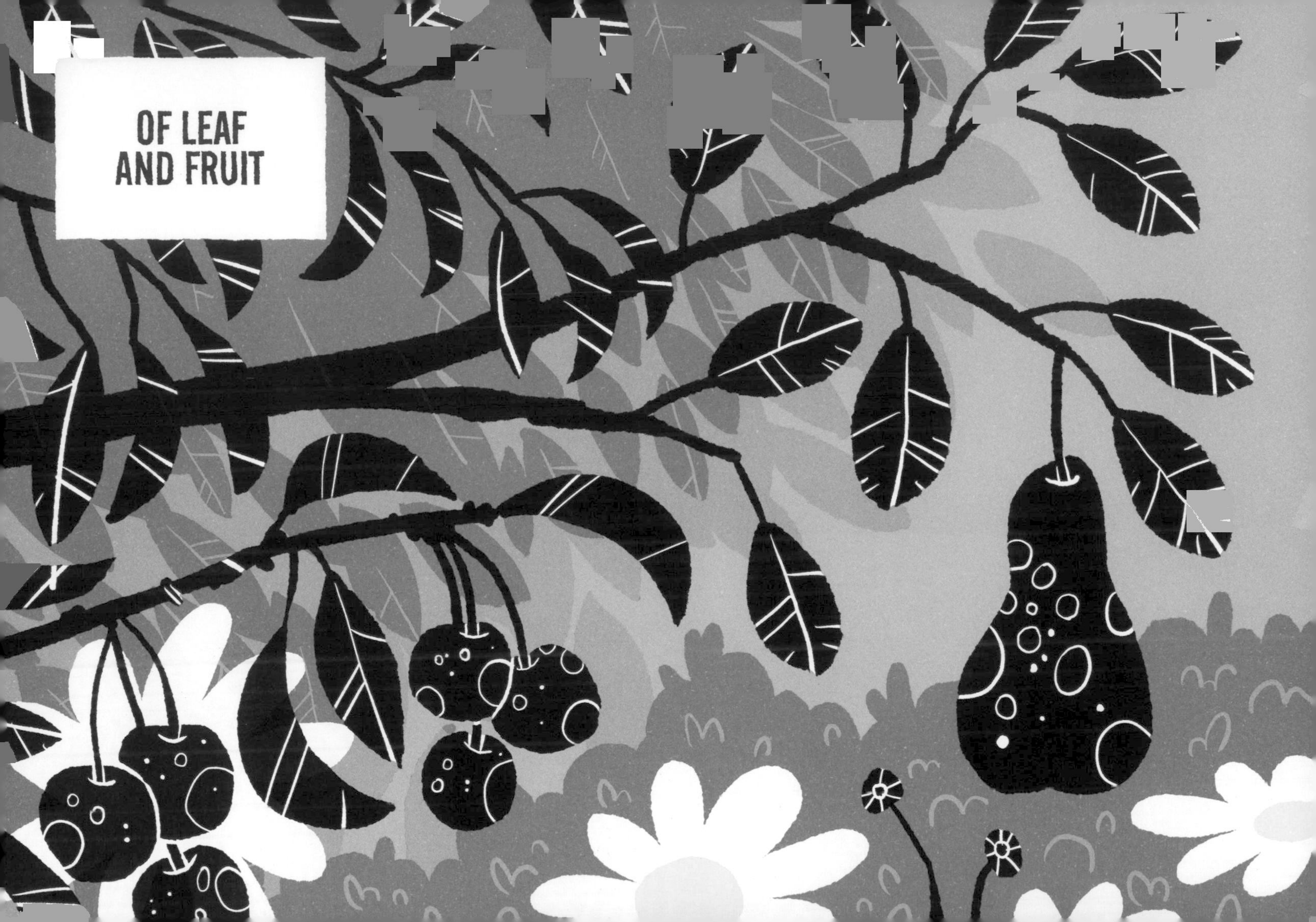

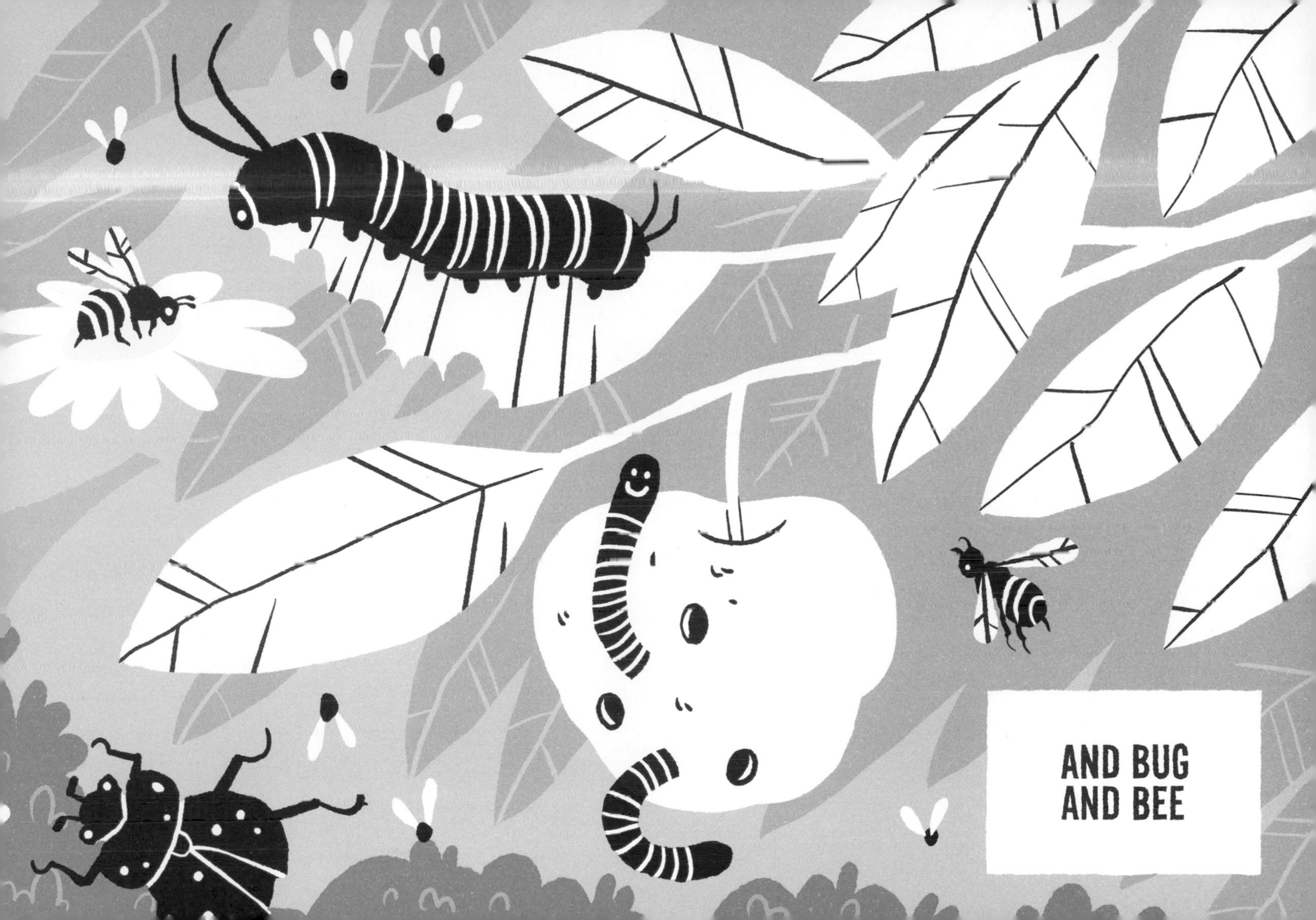

AND BUG
AND BEE

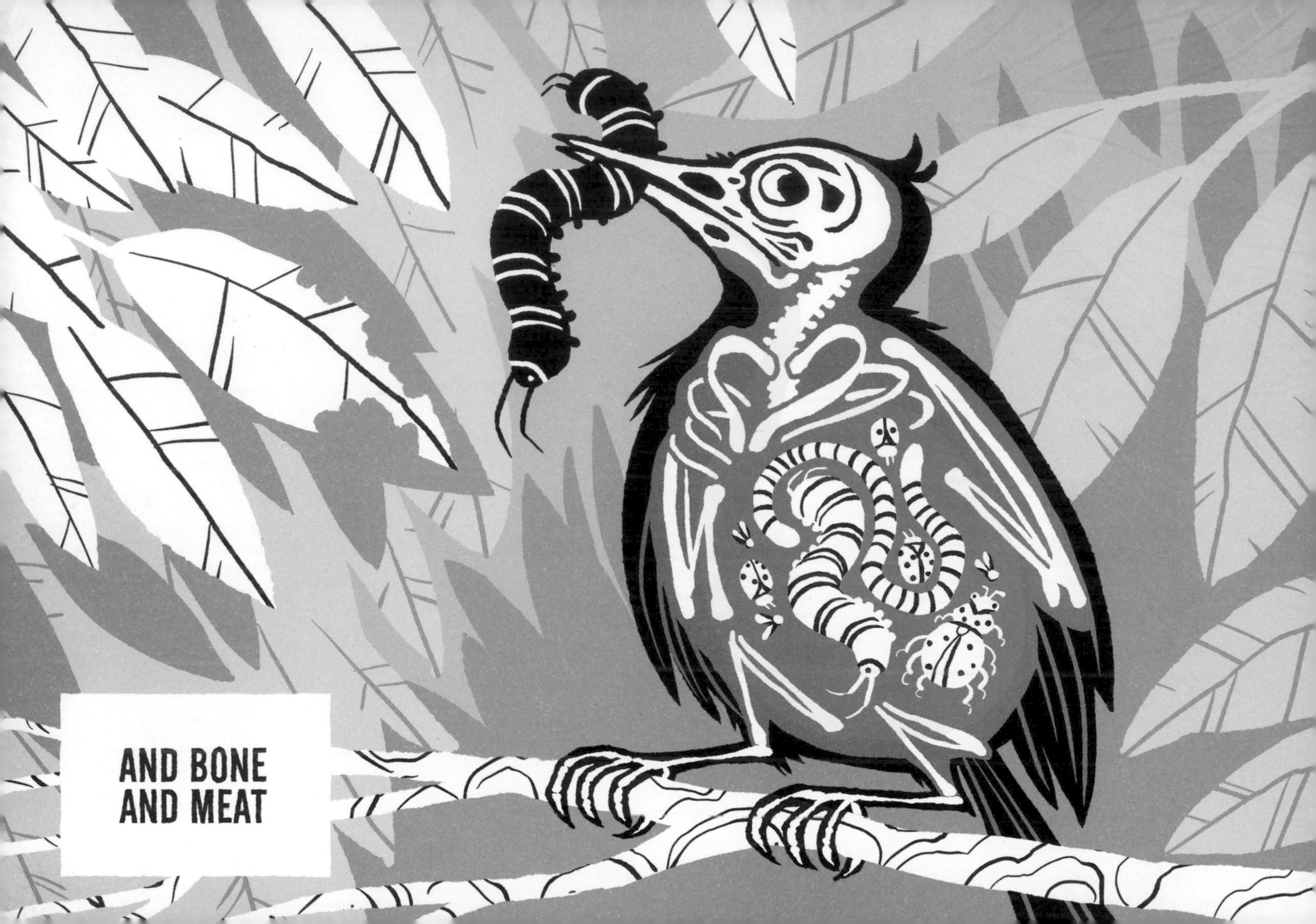
AND BONE
AND MEAT

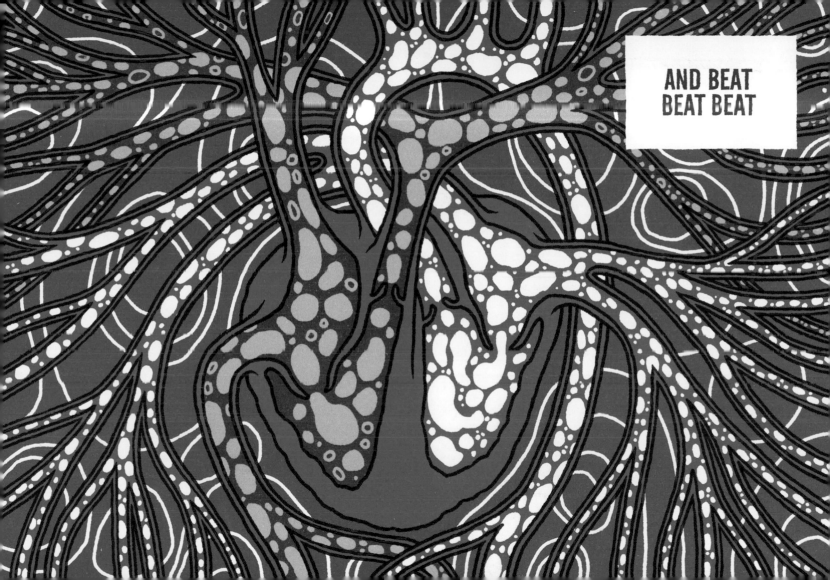

AND BEAT
BEAT BEAT

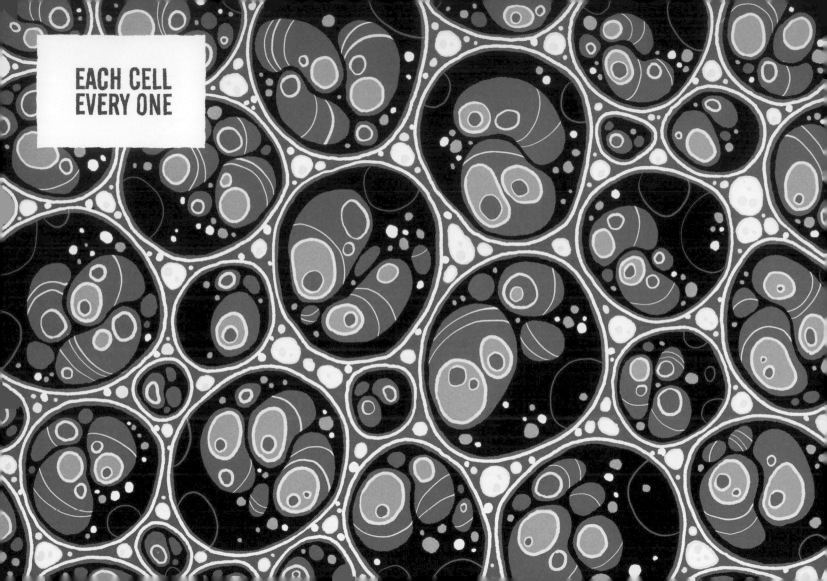

EACH CELL
EVERY ONE

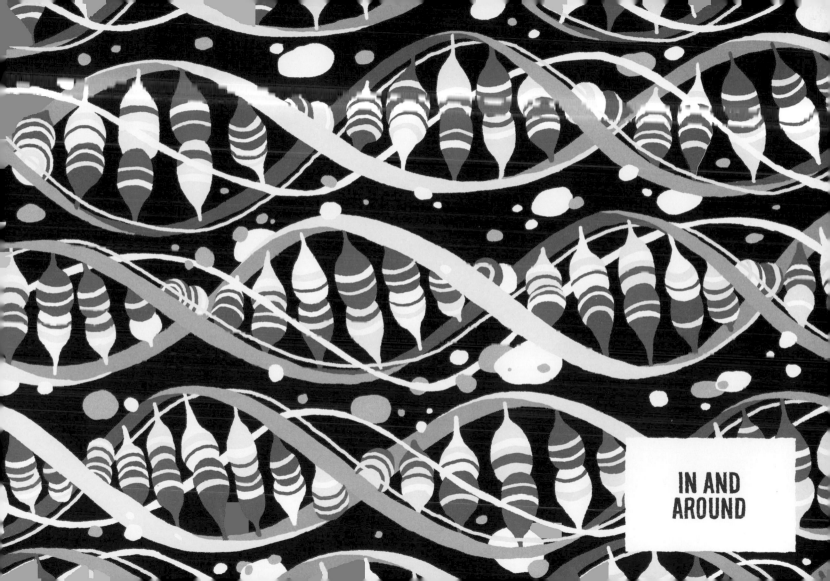

IN AND
AROUND

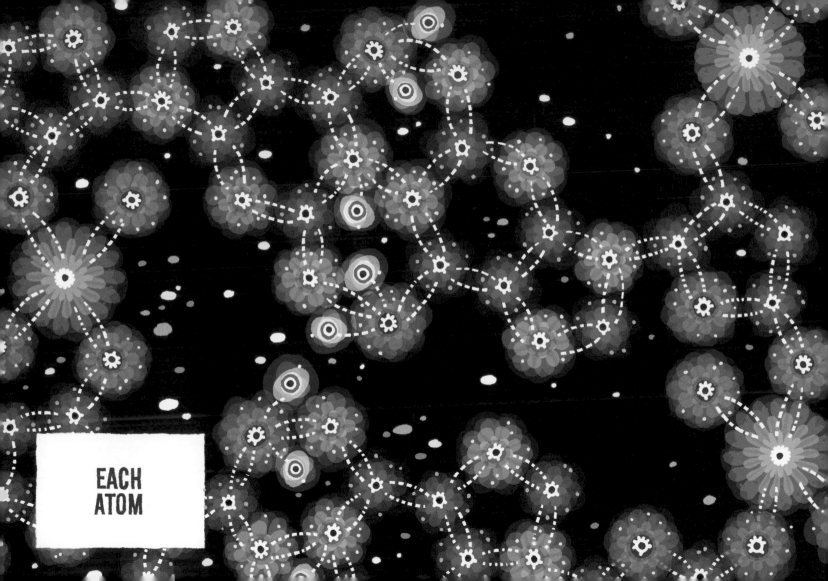

EACH
ATOM

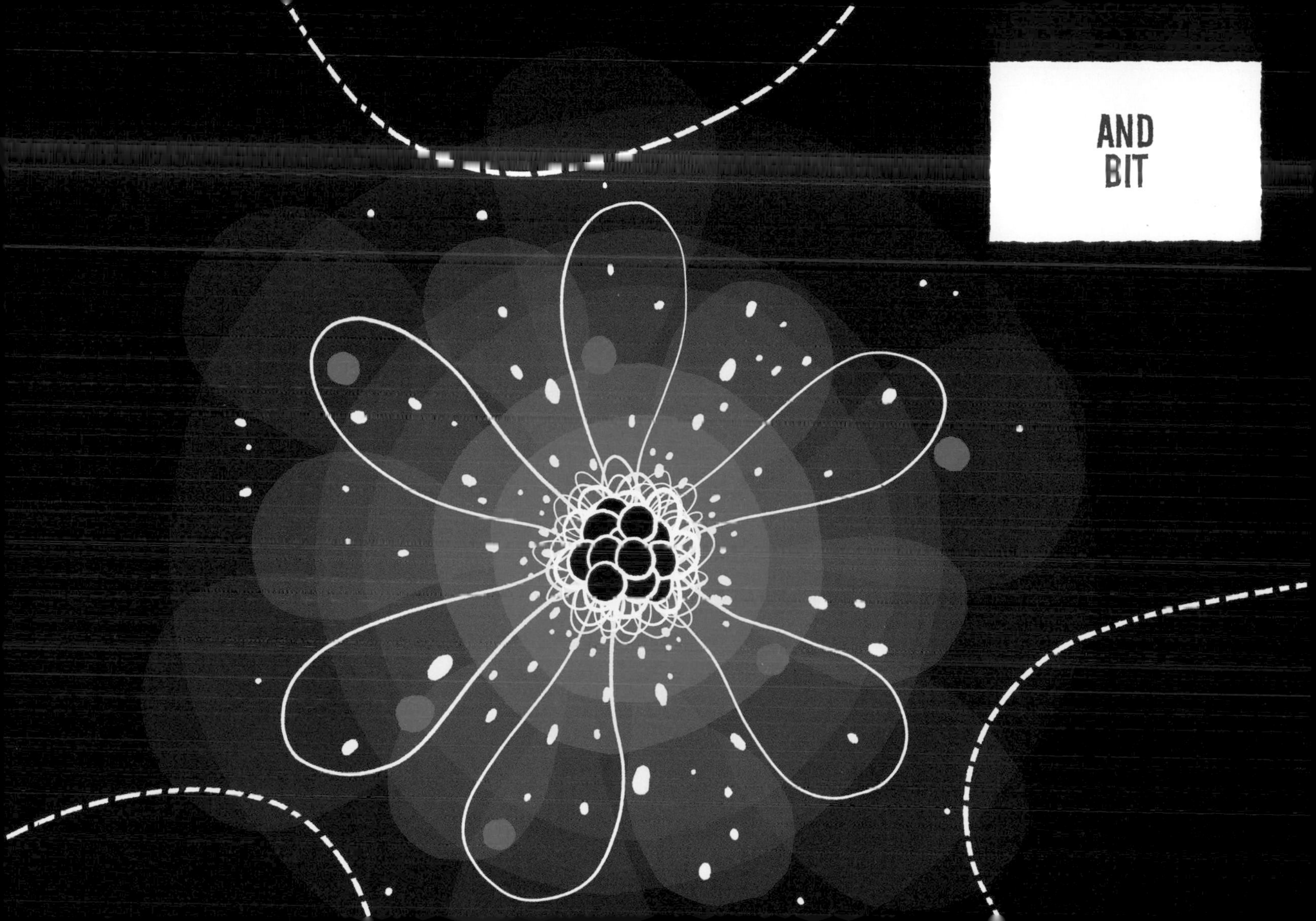
AND
BIT

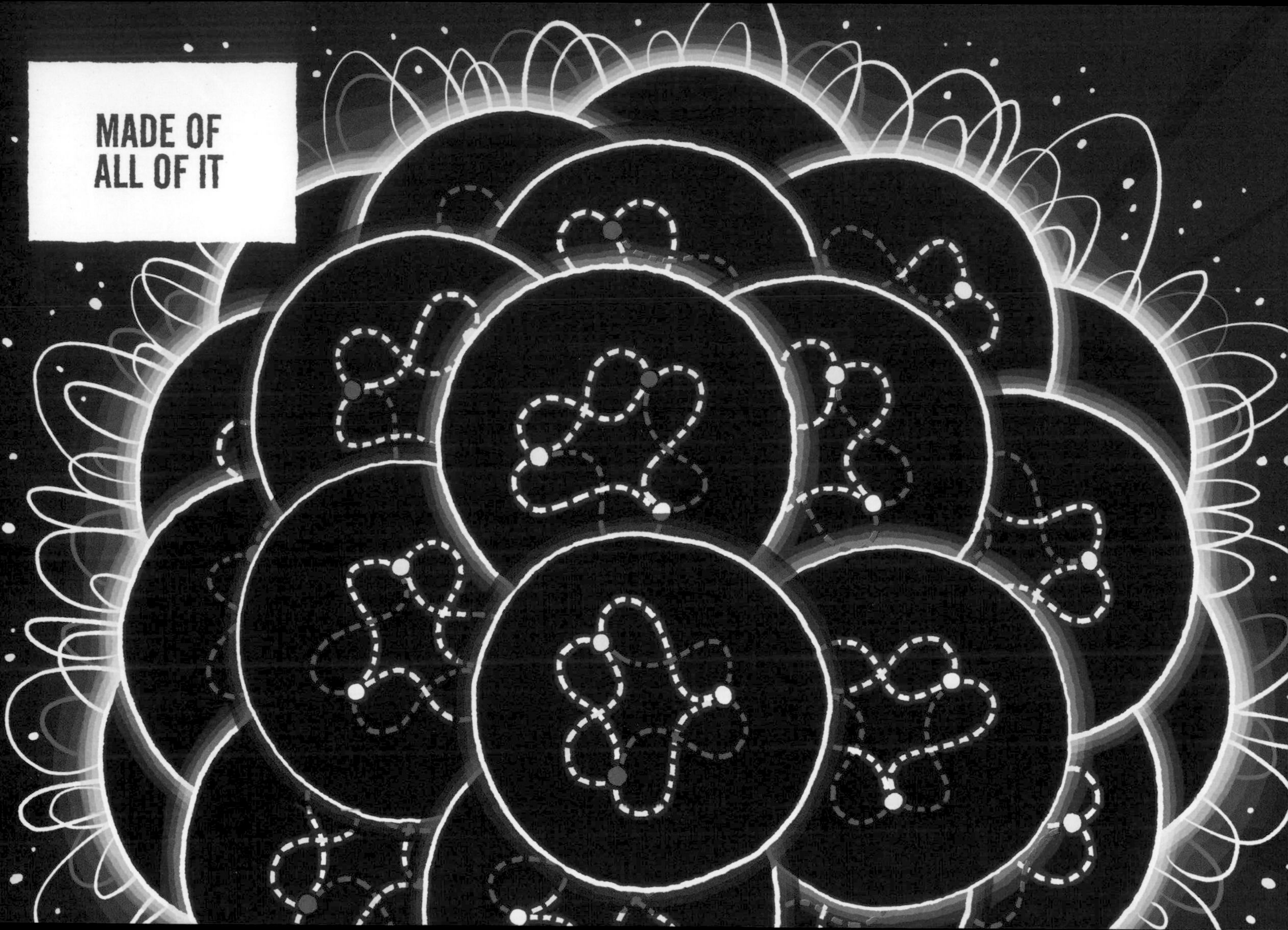
MADE OF
ALL OF IT

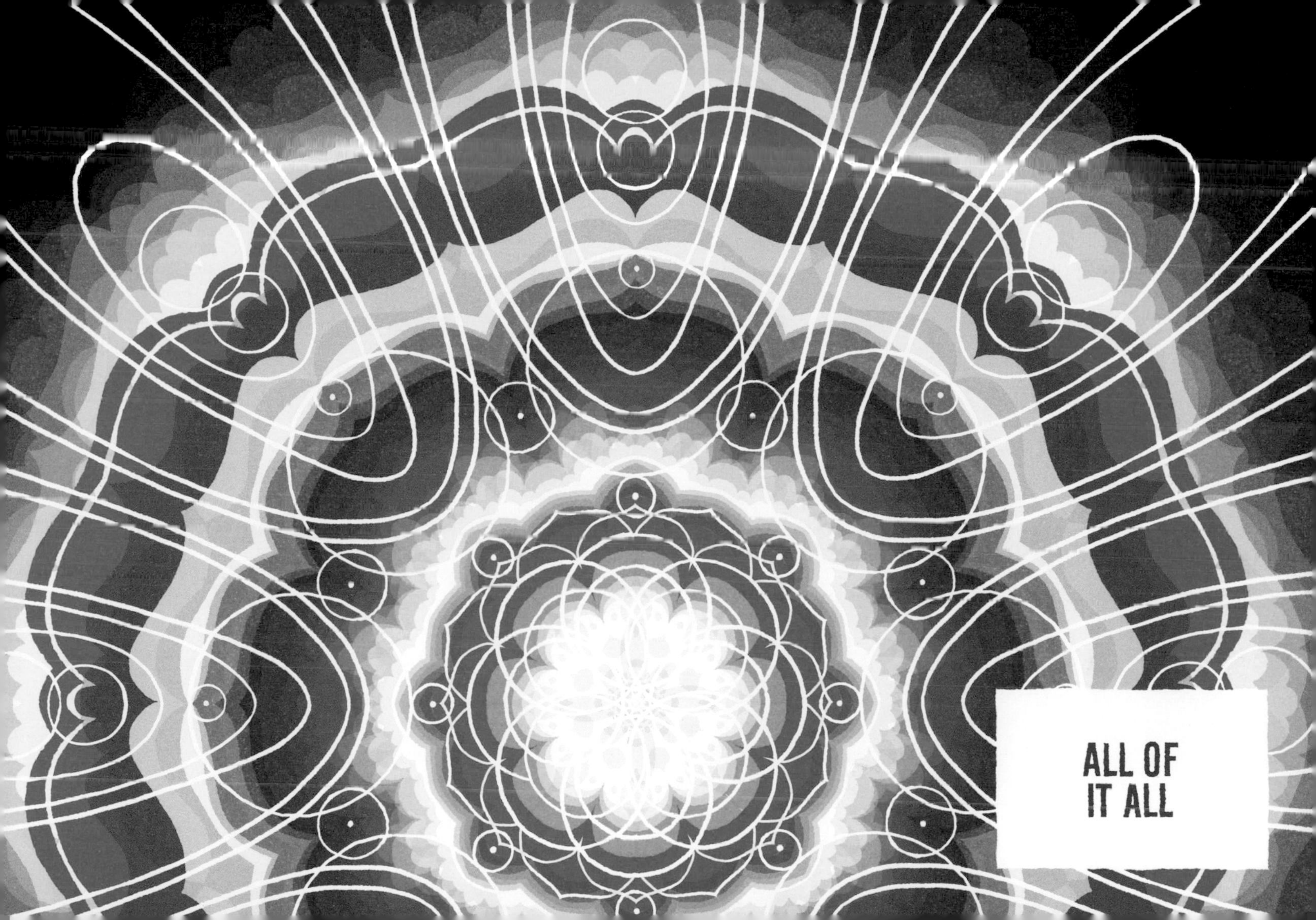
ALL OF
IT ALL

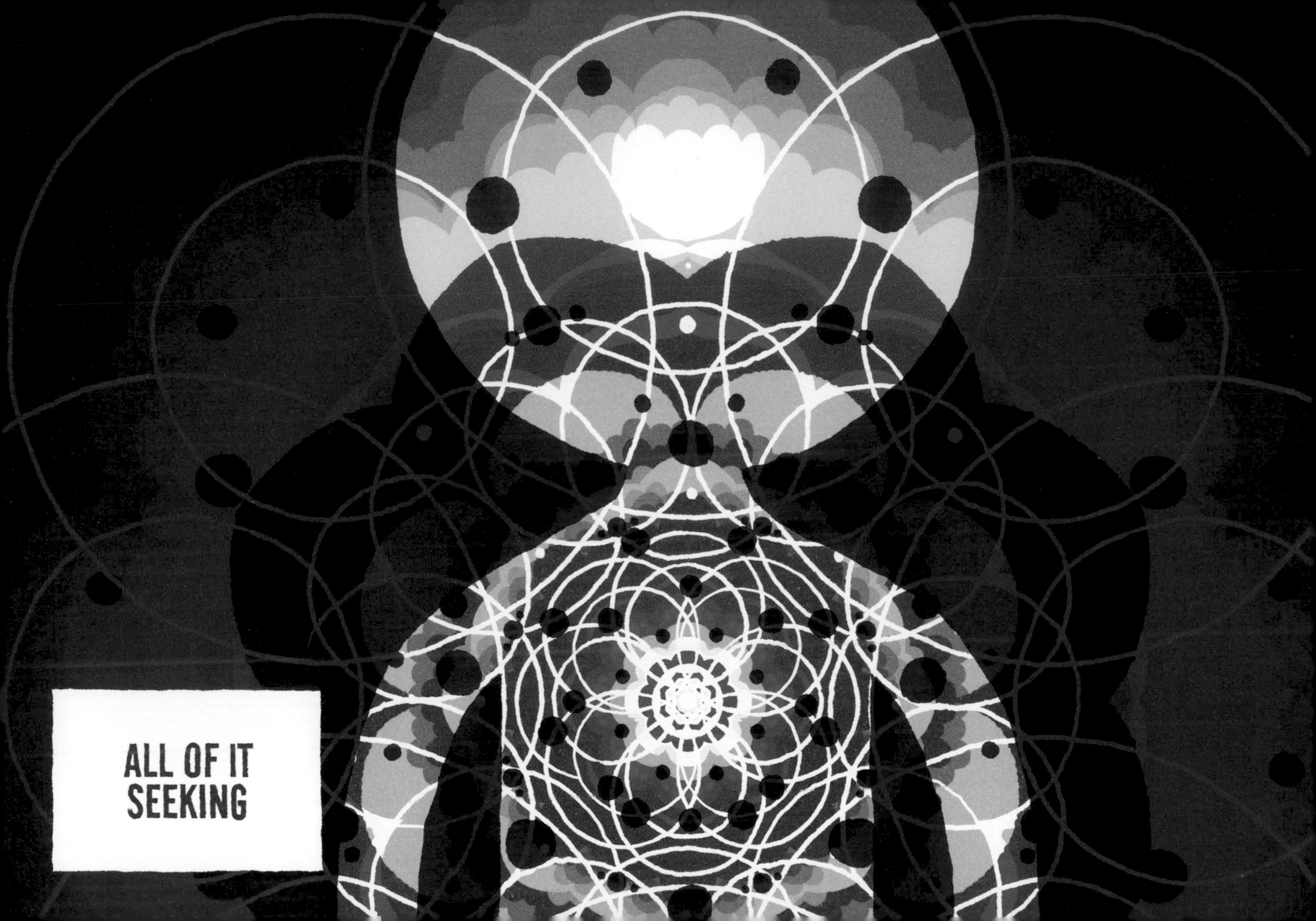
ALL OF IT SEEKING

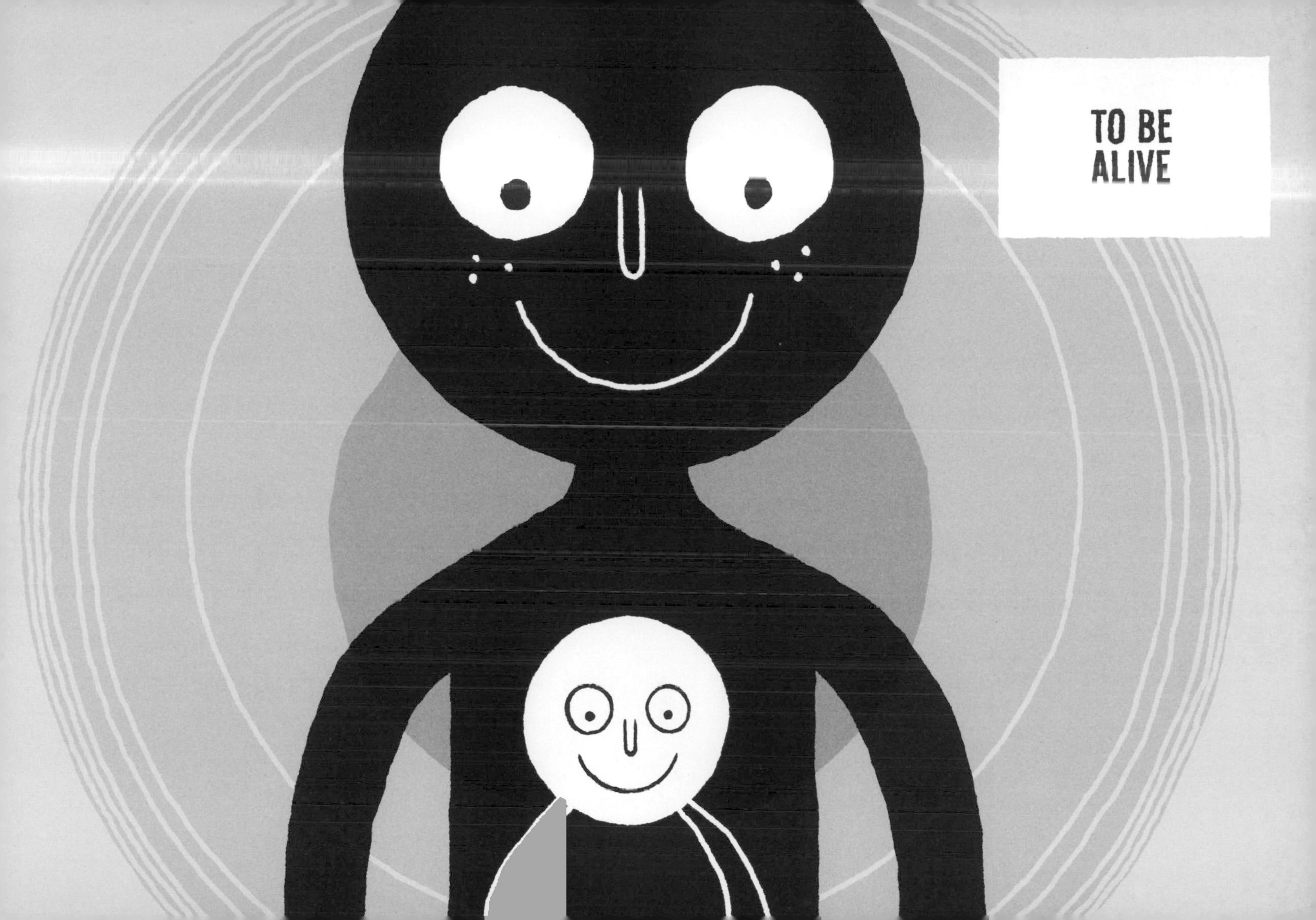

TO BE
ALIVE

TO BE AWARE

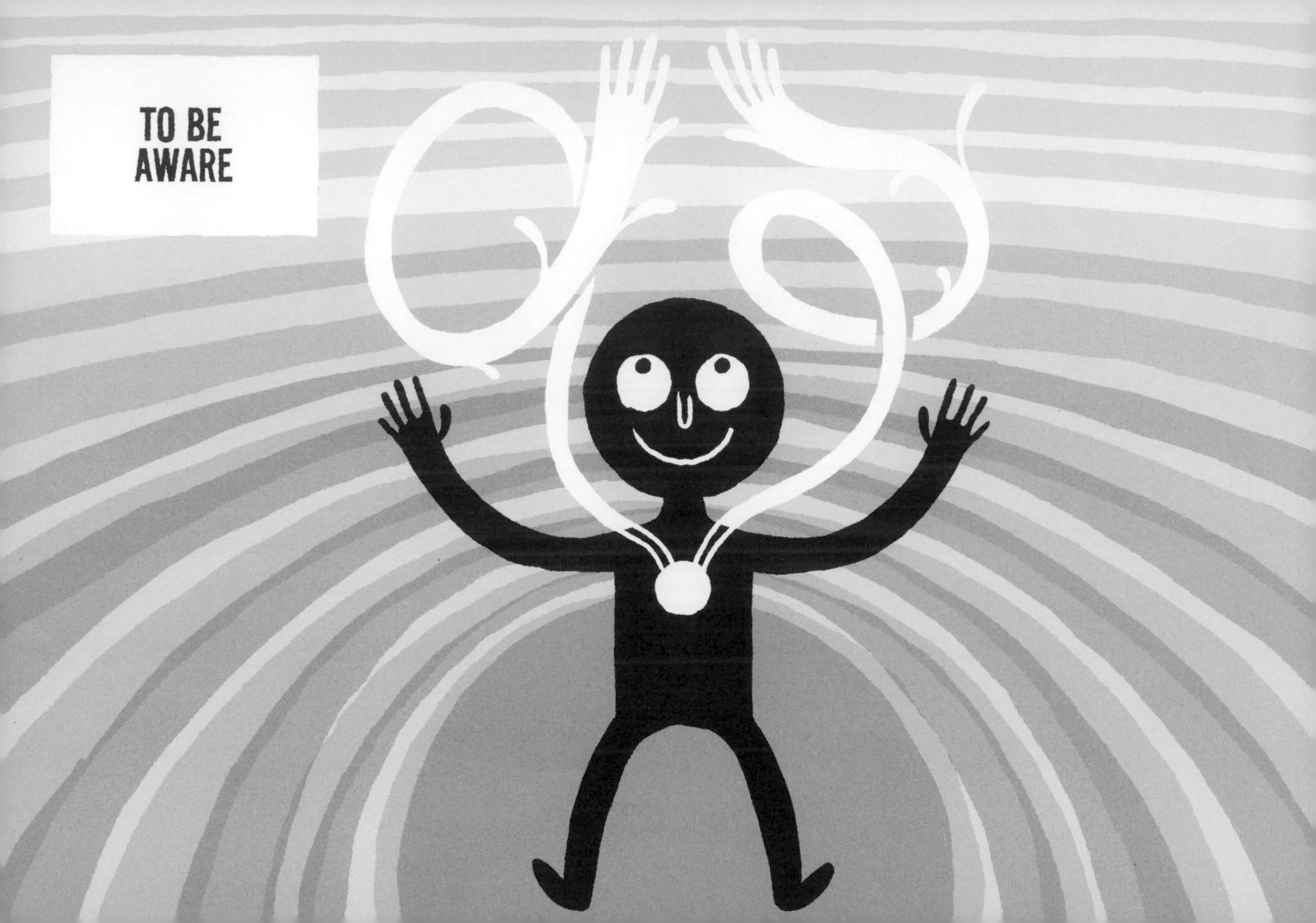

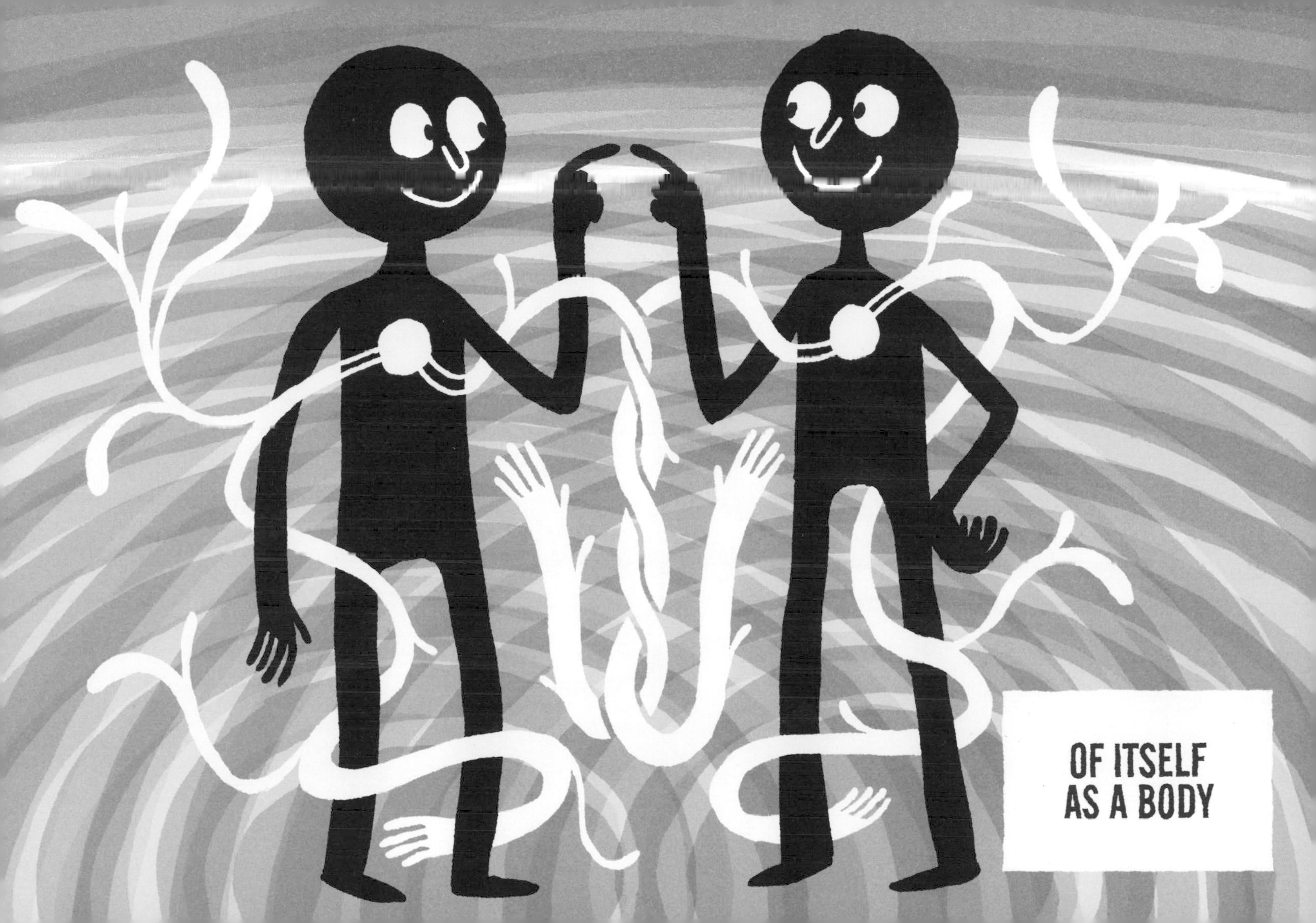
OF ITSELF
AS A BODY

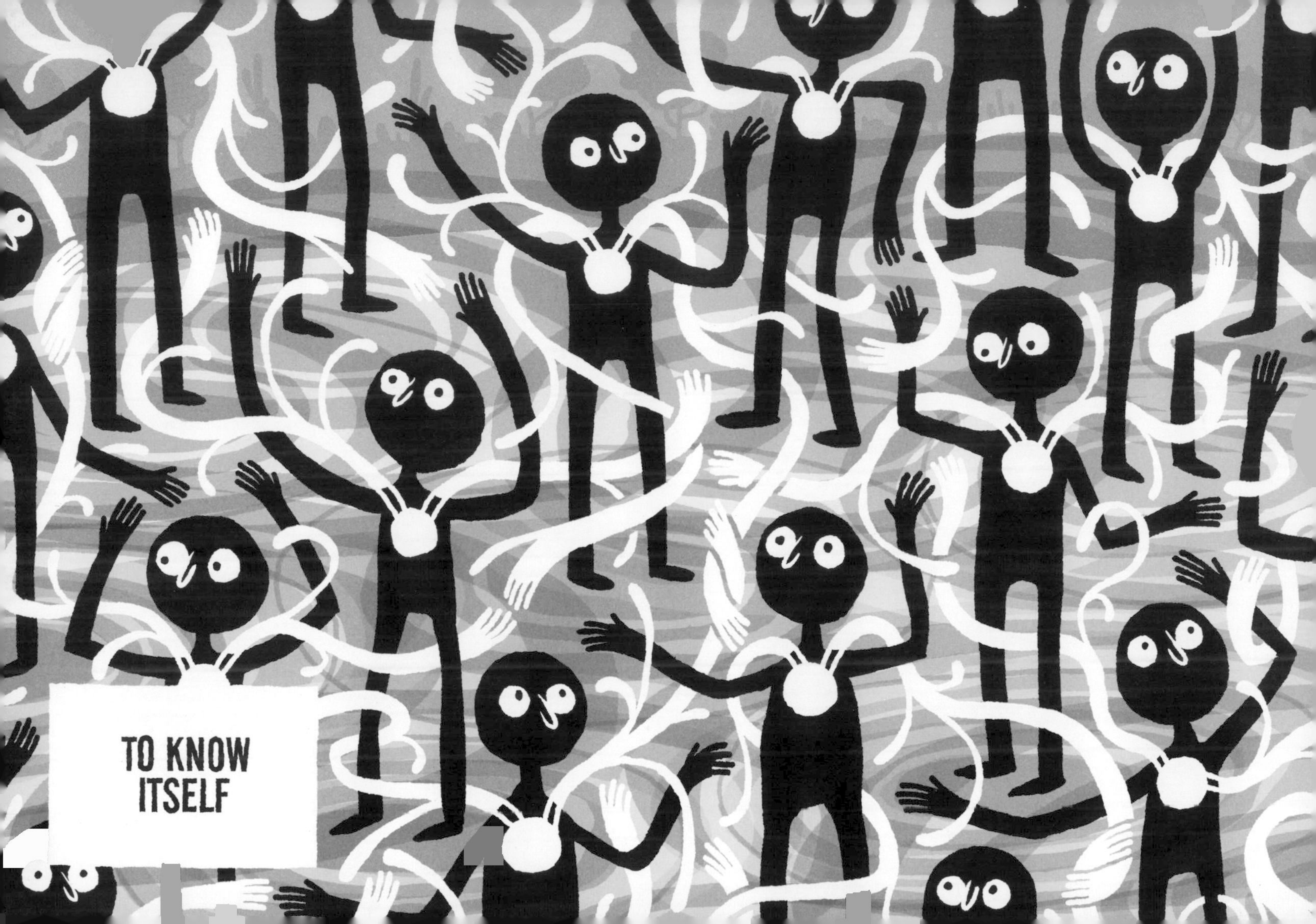
TO KNOW
ITSELF

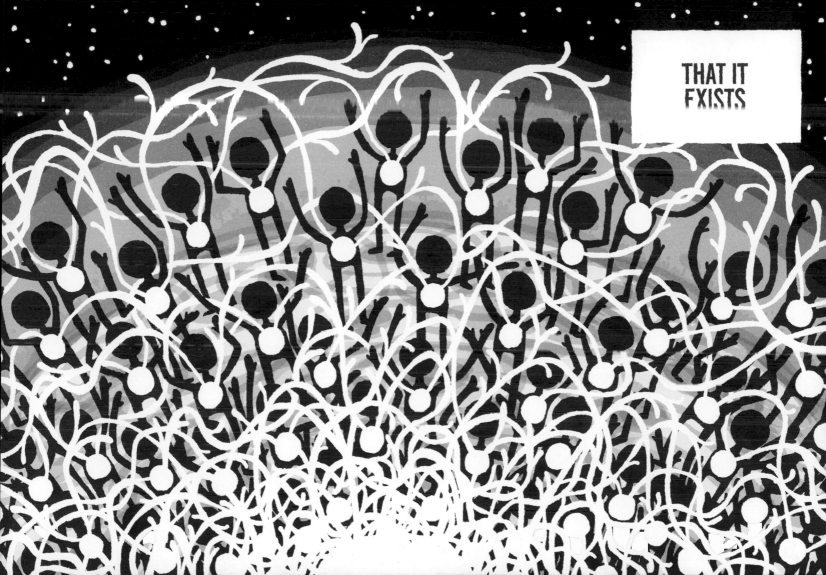

THAT IT
EXISTS

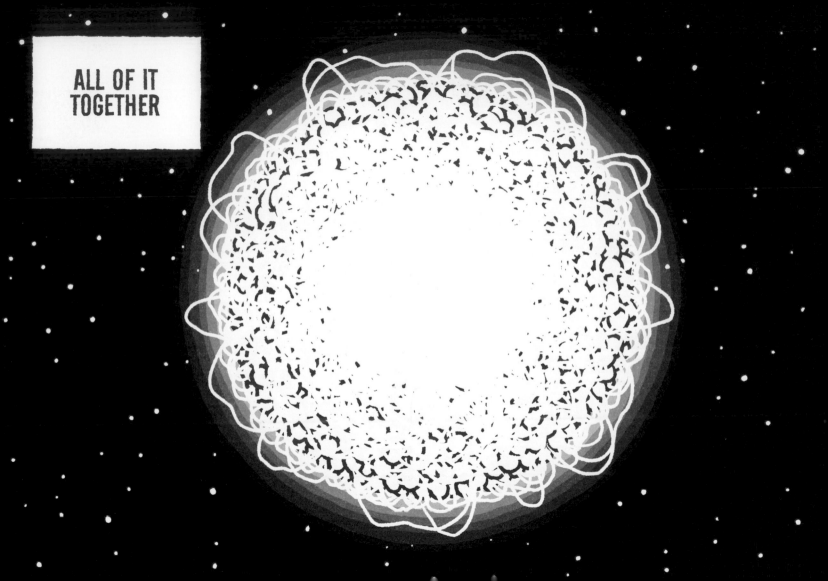

ALL OF IT
TOGETHER

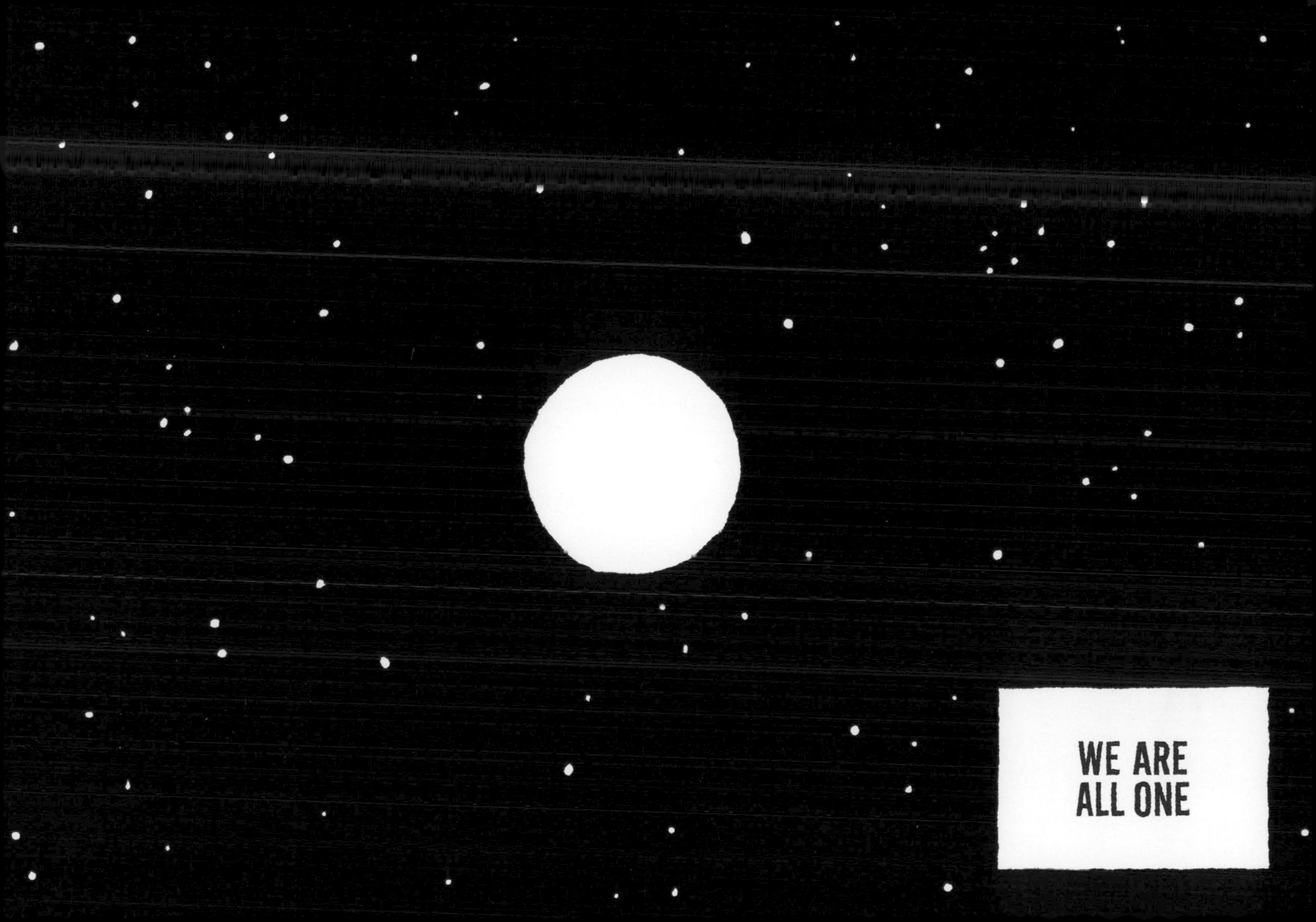
WE ARE
ALL ONE

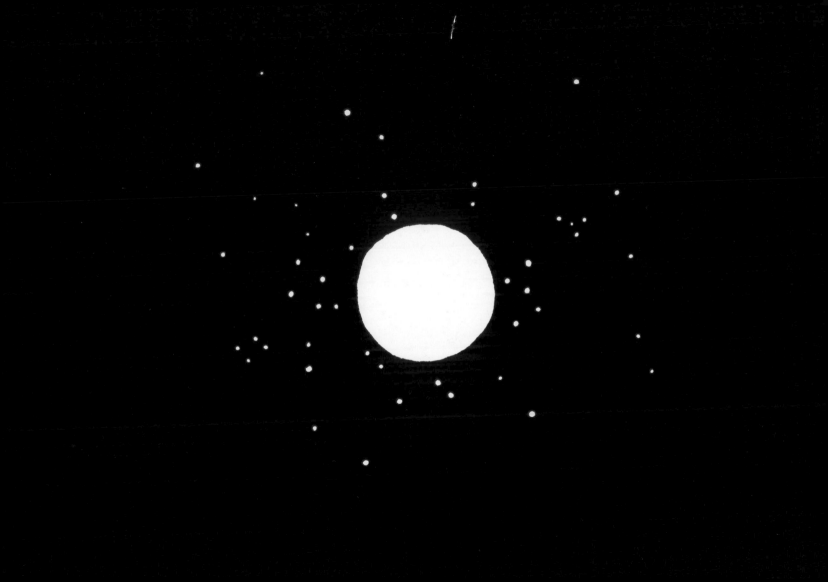